Native Pollinators

Beetles

Roberta
Baxter

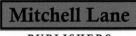

Mitchell Lane

PUBLISHERS

2001 SW 31st Avenue
Hallandale, FL 33009
www.mitchelllane.com

First Edition, 2020.

Author: Roberta Baxter
Designer: Ed Morgan
Editor: Sharon F. Doorasamy

Names/credits:
Title: Beetles / by Roberta Baxter
Description: Hallandale, FL :
Mitchell Lane Publishers, [2020]

Series: Native Pollinators

Library bound ISBN: 9781680203769

eBook ISBN: 9781680203776

Photo credits: www.flaticon.com, freepik.com, Shutterstock.com

Contents

Beetles are amazing! They roamed the Earth before dinosaurs. They helped the first flowers to grow.

Spotted cucumber beetle

Plants sprout from seeds. Flowers appear as plants grow. Flowers need to swap pollen with each other to grow seeds.

Pollen is a powder found in flowers. Beetles and other insects carry pollen from one flower to another. This is called **pollination**.

Beetles eat pollen. The pollen sticks to their bodies. After eating, the beetles fly or crawl to another flower. The pollen falls off of the beetles. It falls onto the new flower. That flower is **pollinated**. The flower turns into seeds. The seeds grow into new plants.

Soldier beetle

11

Beetles prefer flowers shaped like bowls. They like spicy and fruity flowers. They like smelly ones too. Magnolia flowers are favorites. They are big and white. Beetles also pollinate many kinds of palm trees.

Beetles come in a lot of colors. They can be yellow, green, or red. They can have spots or stripes. Most beetles can fly. Fireflies and June bugs are beetles. So are ladybugs.

Some beetles are pests. Bark beetles kill trees in forests. The boll weevil kills cotton plants. Beetles eat parts of the flowers too. They even poop in the flowers.

Boll weevil

Not all beetles are pests. Some are helpful. The ladybug beetle is a helper. Farmers use them to eat insects that damage their crops and fruit trees.

Ladybug

Beetles make up half of all insects in the world. America is home to lots of native beetles. They pollinate flowers on the pawpaw tree. Pawpaw is a fruit. The tree is native to America.

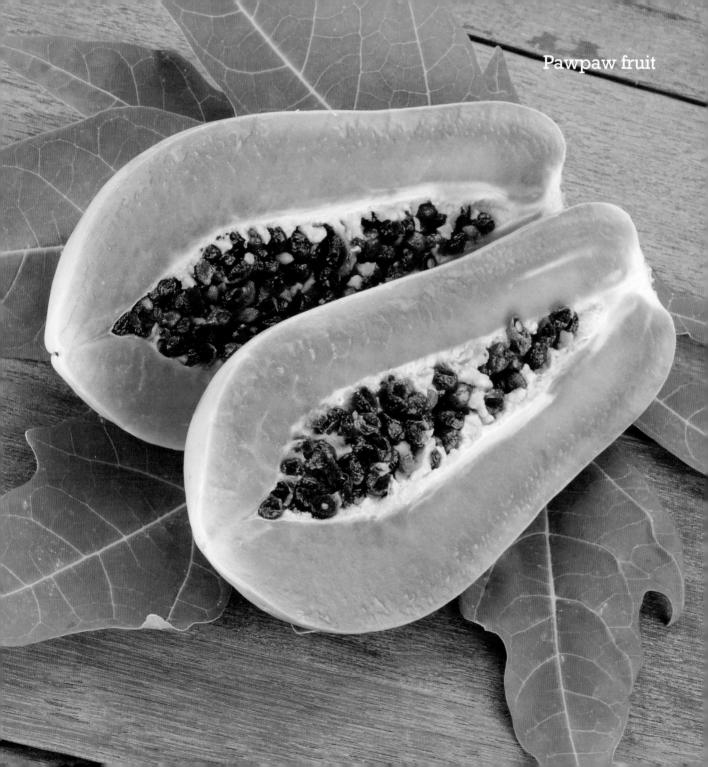

Pawpaw fruit

MAIN BODY PARTS OF A *Beetle*

Beetles have three main body parts. The head includes the eyes that can see all around. The wings and legs are attached to the **thorax**. The **abdomen** is the back part of the beetle.

Beetles have two sets of wings. The front set is called the **forewing**. It covers the second set of wings. Some beetles do not have wings. They only crawl. Beetles have two sets of wings like other insects, such as bees and butterflies. But beetle wings are different. The first set of wings is made of a hard shell. Those wings are not used for flying. They protect the flying wings by folding over them. When the beetle flies, the hard wings move out of the way. The thinner wings stretch out to fly.

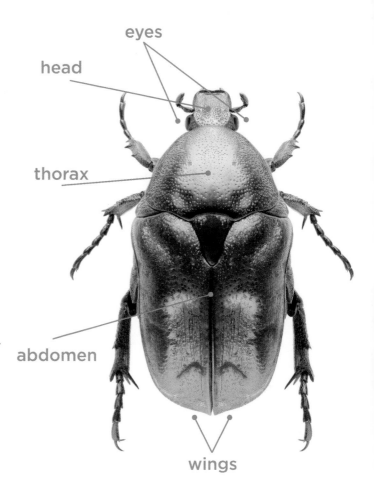

eyes

head

thorax

abdomen

wings

GLOSSARY

abdomen
The back part of a beetle which has the heart and intestines

crops
Plants grown to be used as food

forewing
The front set of wings that a beetle has

native
A beetle that has lived in America from the earliest times; not from another country

pest
An insect that causes damage to plants

pollen
A powder found inside flowers

pollinate
To take pollen from one flower and take it to another flower which allows that flower to turn into fruit

pollination
A process where pollen is spread

thorax
Middle part of a mosquito that holds the wings and the legs

FURTHER READING

Aston, Dianna Hutts, and Sylvia Long. *A Beetle is Shy*. San Francisco: Chronicle Books, 2016.

Jenkin, Steve. *The Beetle Book*. Boston: Houghton Mifflin Books for Children, 2012.

Ipcizade, Catherine. *Breathtaking Beetles*. North Mankato, MN: Capstone Press, 2017.

Rattini, Kristin Baird. *National Geographic Readers: Seed to Plant.* Washington, DC: *National Geographic* Children's Books, 2014.

ON THE INTERNET

http://ucanr.edu/sites/PollenNation/Meet_The_Pollinators/Beetles/
This web site has vivid pictures of beetles on plants and short sections of explanation.

https://learning-center.homesciencetools.com/article/learn-about-beetles/
A section of text about beetles, how they get their name, and other facts is on this site.

https://pestworldforkids.org/pest-guide/beetles/
This site has facts about beetles and descriptions of specific kinds of beetles.

https://www.youtube.com/watch?v=6ON9W5uxgu8
You'll find a video about different types of beetles and where they are found on this site.

INDEX

ABOUT THE AUTHOR

Ladybird beetles and June bugs have always fascinated Roberta Baxter. She lives in Colorado and has written books about science and history for students of all ages. She enjoys the mountains of Colorado in all seasons.